Ronnie Wilson's Gift

Francis Chan

Illustrated by Jim Madsen

David C Cook

transforming lives together

RONNIE WILSON'S GIFT
Published by David C Cook
4050 Lee Vance View
Colorado Springs, CO 80918 U.S.A.

David C Cook Distribution Canada
55 Woodslee Avenue, Paris, Ontario, Canada N3L 3E5

David C Cook U.K., Kingsway Communications
Eastbourne, East Sussex BN23 6NT, England

David C Cook and the graphic circle C logo
are registered trademarks of Cook Communications Ministries.

LCCN 2010940570
ISBN 978-0-7814-0477-8
eISBN 978-0-7814-0597-3

Text © 2011 Francis Chan
Illustrations © James Madsen
Published in association with the literary agency of
D.C. Jacobson & Associates LLC, an Author Management Company
www.dcjacobson.com

The Team: Don Pape, Kate Etue, Amy Kiechlin, Jack Campbell
Cover and Interior Illustrations: Jim Madsen

Manufactured in Shen Zhen, Guang Dong, P.R. China, in December 2010 by Printplus Limited.
First Edition 2011

1 2 3 4 5 6 7 8 9 10

112210

To my dear friend Ron Wilson ... a very wise old man
who still has the faith of a child.

Little Ronnie Wilson's jaw dropped in amazement. It was the first time he'd heard the real reason Jesus came to Earth such a long time ago.

"He did that for us? That's amazing!"

Then an exciting idea popped into Ronnie's mind. "Jesus gave me an awesome gift, so I want to give Him a present too!"

When Ronnie got home, he tried to think of the *perfect* present for Jesus.

His teddy bear? ... was old and falling apart.

His piggy bank? … only had six dollars and forty-seven cents in it.

Then Ronnie saw his baseball glove on his bookshelf. It was signed by his uncle Jack, a player in the big leagues. Ronnie loved his glove more than anything else he owned.

He thought to himself, *Jesus gave me the greatest gift of all, so I want to give Him the greatest gift I can.*

So Ronnie grabbed his glove and raced on his bike to the post office.

"How much will it cost to mail this to heaven? I only have six dollars and forty-seven cents," Ronnie explained.

The mailman answered, "I'm sorry, Ronnie, but we can't deliver mail to heaven. We have no way to get it there."

"Okay, thanks anyway," Ronnie said as he walked out the door.

Ronnie rode home on his bike, thinking of different ways to get his baseball glove to Jesus, when he nearly ran right into a man shuffling down the sidewalk.

"Sorry, sir."

"That's okay, son." The man smiled just a little bit, and Ronnie heard his tummy grumble.

"Um, have you had lunch yet?" Ronnie asked the man.

The man shook his head, and Ronnie thought maybe he didn't have enough money to buy lunch. So Ronnie shook his piggy bank until some coins fell out.

Ronnie gave the money to the man, who used it to buy a hot dog … with the works!

Later, Ronnie went out to his backyard to jump on his trampoline. He jumped as high as he could. In fact, he jumped so high that his next-door neighbor, Jesse, saw him.

"What are you doing?" Jesse asked.

"I'm trying to jump to heaven so I can give my baseball glove to Jesus. Do you want to jump with me?" Ronnie asked.

Jesse said, "Yes!"

Jesse and Ronnie didn't jump high enough to make it to heaven, but they had a good time trying.

At the carnival the next day, Ronnie bought a giant balloon with the rest of his money. Then he tied his baseball glove to the balloon and wrote a note to Jesus.

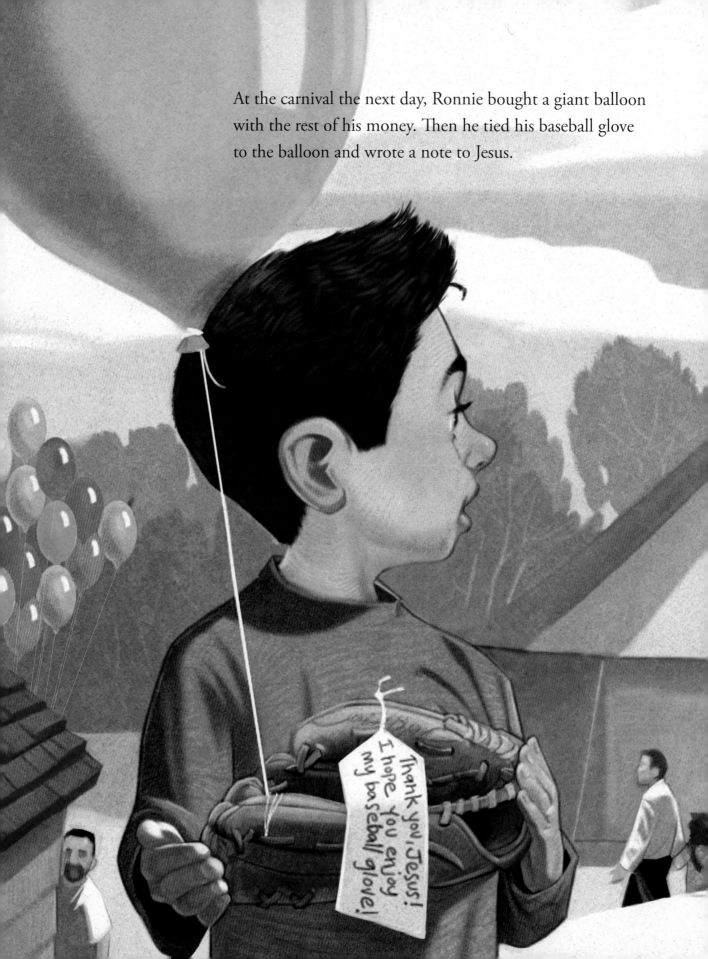

Just as he was about to let his balloon fly up to heaven, he heard a little girl crying, "Mommy! My balloon!"

Ronnie didn't like that the little girl was sad, so he gave his balloon to her. But now he had no way to get his gift to Jesus. Ronnie prayed, "Jesus, I'm so sorry I couldn't get Your present to You. I tried my hardest. Thank You anyway."

That night, Ronnie had the strangest dream. He was in heaven, and Jesus said
to him, "Thanks for the present, Ronnie!"

"What present?"

"Thanks for the balloon when I was sad. Thanks for jumping on the trampoline
with me when I was lonely. And thanks for the hot dog when I was hungry."

"What do you mean?" Ronnie asked.

Jesus answered, "Don't you remember what I wrote in the Bible? Whatever you do for these brothers of Mine, you do for Me.

"Billy is the man you saw near the post office. He lost everything in a fire, except his faith. He had just prayed for food, and I used you to answer his prayer.

"Your neighbor, Jesse, loves Me, but he is lonely. I used you to be a friend to him.

"And the little girl who lost her balloon … her name is Rachel. Her dad works hard but doesn't have a lot of money. So I loved it when you gave her your balloon.

"They are all My children, and when you give a gift to My children in need, it's the same as giving to Me! So thanks, Ronnie!"

Just then, Ronnie woke up. It was the happiest dream he'd ever had, and he wore a huge smile across his face. Now he knew exactly what he was going to do.

Later that day, Ronnie went to play at the park with his friend Keith. Keith had always wanted to play on a baseball team, but he didn't have a glove. So that afternoon, Ronnie gave him a surprise present. Keith had never been so excited!

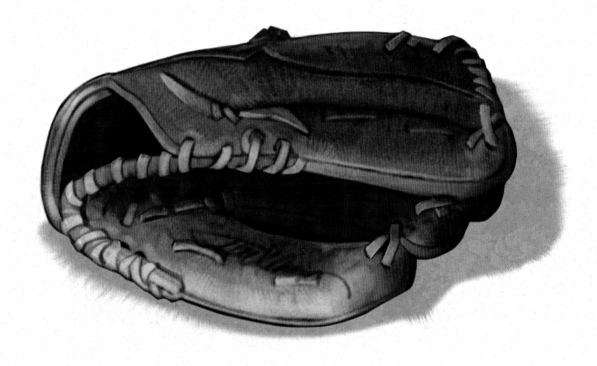

As Ronnie knelt by his bed that night, he looked up to heaven and whispered, "Jesus, I hope You enjoy the baseball glove."

"And the King will answer them, 'Truly, I say to you, as you did it to one of the least of these my brothers, you did it to me'" (Matthew 25:40).

Dear Parent,

Because you have this book in your hands, it is pretty safe to assume that you care a lot about your child's relationship with God. When my first child was born, I remember carrying my little baby around the house regularly and praying the same prayer over and over: "God, please have her fall in love with You!" Sound familiar?

It is now fifteen years later, and during those years the Lord has blessed me with three more children. A lot has changed in my life, but what remains the same is my tremendous concern that my children walk with Jesus. I still pray for them daily. In addition to that, I take seriously my responsibility to teach them and to live in such a way that they learn about Jesus just by watching my life.

It is our responsibility as parents to be the primary teachers of God's Word to our children. Too often, parents depend on Sunday school teachers, youth pastors, or counselors to train up their children. While God will use others to influence our kids, it is His design that we parents are the primary teachers (Deuteronomy 6:4–25; Ephesians 6:4). You probably noticed that I began the story with Ronnie amazed by the gospel, but I did not explain the gospel at that point. I did this in order to give you the freedom and responsibility to explain the story of Christ to your child. Jesus and the apostles shared the good news differently based on the audience. Since you know your children best, you would probably do the best job teaching them the gospel.

God calls parents not only to talk about Jesus, but also to live like Him (1 John 2:6; 1 Corinthians 11:1). As the old expression goes, "Most lessons are caught, not taught." Our kids are watching us and will remember our actions more than our words. I hope you use this story as a teaching tool for your children, but they will learn the greatest lesson as they watch their parents give generously. My kids have seen my wife and me give to the poor, and they looked on with amazement as they saw the blessings of God that followed. This is the type of lesson they won't soon forget. I pray that as you teach your kids this invaluable lesson of giving generously, God would give you the faith to live it out. Then your kids will see just how blessed we are when we give.

"Whoever is generous to the poor lends to the LORD, and he will repay him for his deed" (Proverbs 19:17).

Serving with you,
Francis